# I Wish I Were a Superhero

By Sarah E. Paul

Illustrated by
Tara Lehning

## Acknowledgements:

Thank you to my husband for listening to me drone on every day about my little book. Thank you to my sister for sharing the book with, I assume, everyone she has ever met. Thank you to my best friend Kristi for lending her stunning graphic design skills to the book so that it could, in fact, be published.

Thank you to Liz for suggesting the main character be a cute animal.
Thank you to Tara for making the book impossibly beautiful.

Thank you to my dad, who years ago suggested one of the verses be about super smarts.

Thank you to my dear friends and family who have kindly supported my first publishing adventure.

This edition's first printing was September 2020

Book layout by Kristi Siedow-Thompson

*For My Dad*

Every night before I sleep,

Before I even climb in bed,

I put on my super cape

And tie a mask around my head.

I leap and dive and somersault

Off all the tables and chairs;

And rescue helpless teddy bears

From my sister's evil lair.

I wish I were a hero

With lots of super powers.

I betcha I could change the world

In just a few short hours.

I could fly through the air

Or even swim through the sea!

They'd shine a light in the sky

So you'd know it was me.

HEY! Wait just a minute!

What kind of hero should I be?

I wish I were a superhero

So I could fly through the air!

I would race the biggest planes

On the tiniest little dare!

I might ZOOM through the sky

And spot a cat in a tree.

Then I'd WOOSH to his rescue,

"No job's too small for me!"

I wish I were a superhero

With lots of great big muscles.

I'd rescue kids from falling rubble

And give their hair a tousle.

I could lift the buildings up

And move them all around.

"Sure thing, mayor, I'll move the school

And build a new playground!"

I wish I were a superhero

With my head all full of brains.

I'd invent gigantic machines

That would put the villains to shame.

When the fighting was done

And the bad guys put away,

I'd rebuild my machines –

Make a pool for my friends to play!

I wish I were a superhero,

The kind that can breathe water.

I'd make friends with mermaids

And race the cute sea otters.

And better yet, when I'd get wet

Would be my greatest power.

No pirates would come plundering

Because I'd give them all a shower.

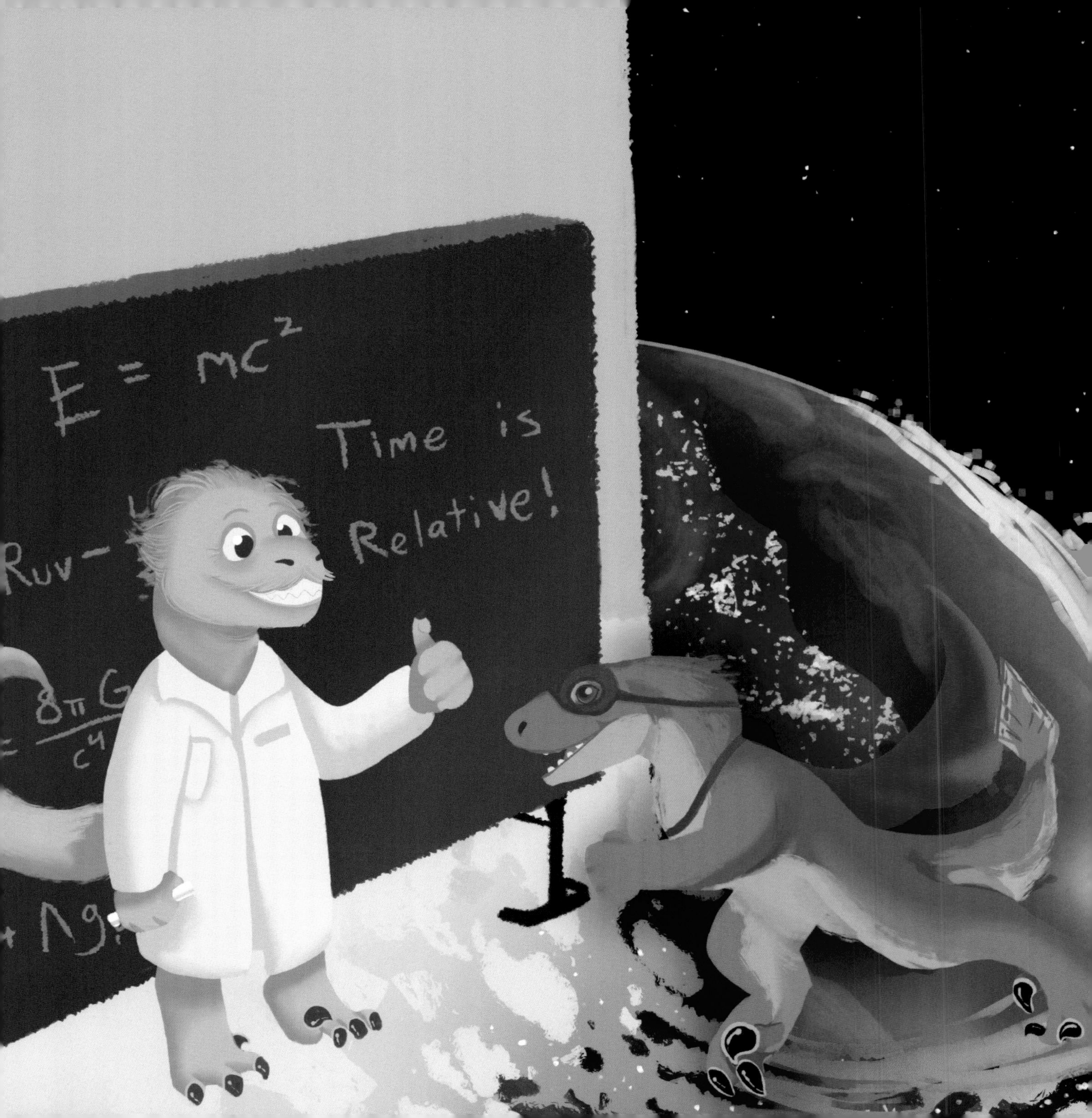
E = mc2
Time is Relative!

I wish I were a superhero

With feet as fast as lightning.

I'd run fast to catch the bad guys

And to them I would be frightening.

I could run around the world,

So fast I'd go through time.

Who knew my feet would help me meet

The genius Albert Einstein!

I wish I were a superhero

And could freeze things with my mind.

Then I'd make some frozen treats

And popsicles all the time!

I could make a giant igloo,

So big, it would make you drool.

It would be my own ice fortress –

"The Fortress of Super Cool."

I wish I were a superhero

And could vanish any time.

I could be invisible –

That's how I'd stop a crime!

They wouldn't no what hit 'em,

Those bad guys when they'd trip

On my outstretched arms and legs,

"You can't give me the slip!"

I wish I were a superhero

With lots of fancy gadgets.

I wouldn't lift a finger

To catch those sneaky bandits!

I could have a secret lair;

Or maybe a fancy car.

Or better yet – a jumbo jet!

– To take me near and far!

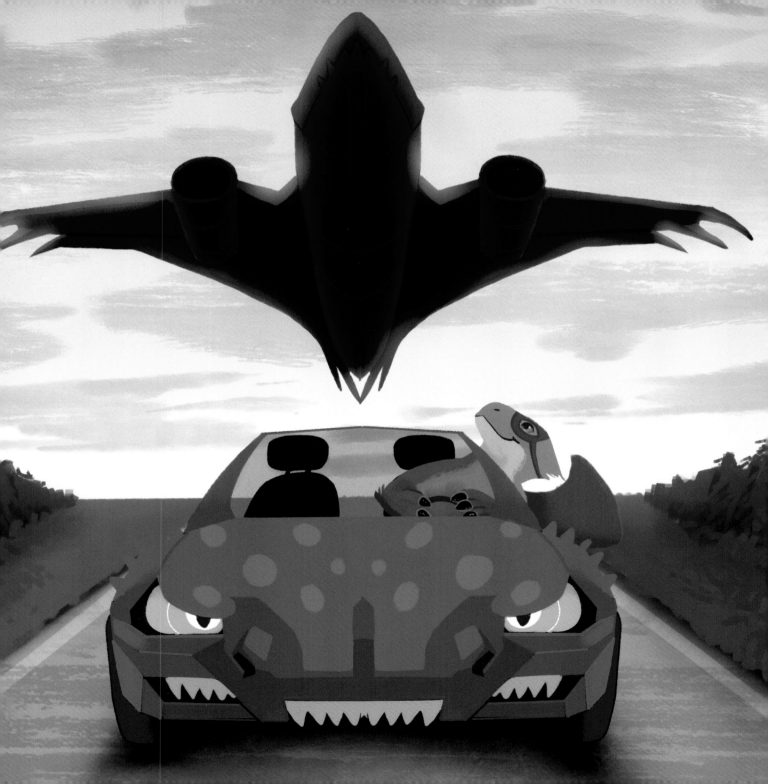

I wish I were a superhero

And could stretch my every limb.

The kids would love when I'd become

A private jungle gym!

I'd stretch my arm to stop a thief;

My leg would stop a bus.

Those sweet old ladies would be so grateful –

They'd make quite a fuss.

I would keep the whole world safe

From danger and destruction.

Every day there'd be a parade

In my honor – what a production!

I wish I were a superhero.

Wouldn't that be great?

Mom says, "Yes, but time for bed.

You know it's getting late."

Rest your head on your pillow;

Close your eyes when you do.

And maybe when you wake up

YOU can make your dreams come true.

# The End

# About The Author

**Sarah E. Paul** is a wife, a performer and a former children's entertainer who enjoys cosplay, roller skating and playing fetch with her dogs. She also really, really loves superheroes. *I Wish I Were A Superhero* is Sarah's first book.

The idea for this book came from Sarah's love of superheroes and her admiration for children's imaginations. Superheroes can show children a limitless amount of possibilities; lots of ways to be strong and do good things. Her hope is that this story will inspire children to explore all of their interests and work hard for their goals. And, of course, remind them that dinosaurs are cool.